TINY TREE
CHILDREN'S BOOKS

First Published 2018

Tiny Tree Children's Books (an imprint of Matthew James Publishing Ltd)

Unit 46, Goyt Mill

Marple

Stockport

SK6 7HX

www.tinytreebooks.com

ISBN: 978-1-910265-58-1

Printed by Chapel Print Ltd
ROCHESTER | www.chapelprint.com

Poppy is a positively perfect penguin,
All dressed in her best coat and tie.
But Pops holds a magical secret,
She is a penguin who can fly!

Now don't get me wrong dear reader,
I know what you think, that I lie.
But honestly, truly and with hand on heart,
Poppy the penguin can fly!

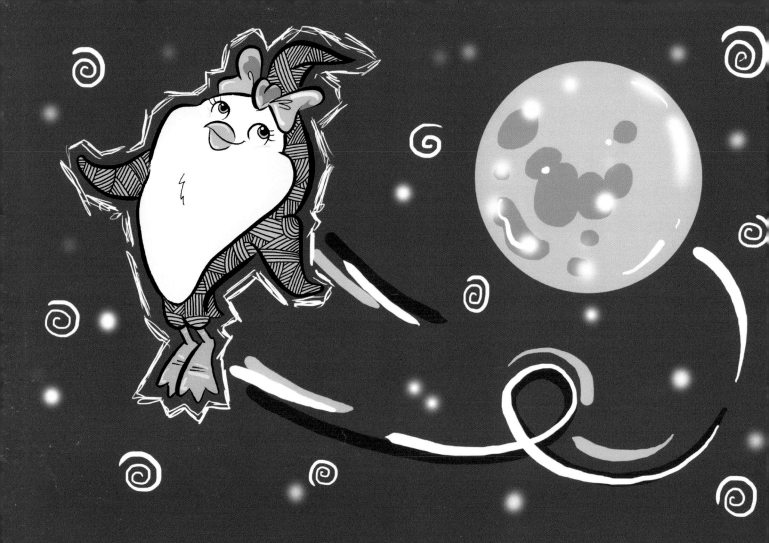

At night she will sneak from her group,
Will run and take off to the sky.
Looping and swirling in the silvery moonlight,
How amazing to watch Poppy fly!

Her flights take her in many directions,
Over oceans with fewer fish to fry.
The fishermen's nets float empty,
Watched by Poppy the penguin who can fly!

On other adventures she heads to the sun,
With deserts all barren and dry.
Children without water or food
Don't notice a penguin fly by.

She sees the dry and sandy farms,
Not a rain-cloud crossing the sky.
No food will grow on this farm today
As Poppy looks down from on high.

She flies over forests and woodlands,
With trees that reach out to the sky.
Chainsaws buzz as land is cleared,
Poppy's not the only bird to fly.

So many other birds made homeless,
They watch their trees fall with a cry.
The forests are now gone forever,
As Poppy says sadly, goodbye.

The city is next to be visited,
With thousands of people rushing by.
Like ants they scuttle and scurry,
No time to watch Poppy fly by.

Cars and machines fill the landscape,
Clouds of gas bring tears to the eye.
Smog and pollution fills the city,
As Poppy is forced to soar high.

Outside of the cities there is rubbish,
Recycling is something they don't try.
Plastic and paper are scattered,
Tossed about as Poppy flies by.

Rubbish is crammed into landfill,
The ground takes it in with a sigh.
More and more holes are getting filled up,
And Poppy flying by just asks why?

Her flights always bring her homeward,
Where the ice lies gleaming and high.
But the sea is warm and the ice melts,
All seen by Poppy who can fly.

Unlike all the other penguins,
Poppy sees the problems that lie.
Her home is quickly disappearing,
A thought that makes poor Poppy cry.

She looks at her land and those she has seen
And tears well up in her eye.
This beautiful place is dying,
But she is sure we can help if we try.

With thought of people and creatures,
And love, something money can't buy,
Poppy is sure we can save Earth,
So she would have no reason to fly.

At the start of this story dear reader
I told you a little white lie.
Only in dreams does Poppy take flight,
In her dreams our penguin can fly

Her flight may be something of fancy,
But the facts she has seen do not lie.
The Earth is our magical planet
That we must protect, you ask why?

Because without this beautiful planet,
With deserts and mountains so high,
Busy cities and beautiful icebergs,
Where else would Poppy have to fly?